It's Been a Pretty Good Ride

Bob Harshbarger

ARPress
45 Dan Road Suite 36
Canton MA 02021

Hotline: 1(800) 220-7660
Fax: 1(855) 752-6001

Ordering Information:
Quantity sales. Special discounts are available on quantity purchases by corporations, associations, and others. For details, contact the publisher at the address above.

ISBN-13:   Paperback   979-8-89389-674-9
            eBook   979-8-89389-675-6

Library of Congress Control Number: 2024922192

DEDICATION

This book is dedicated to my family whose love, inspiration and humor have brought me through many of life's adventures and challenges. A special dedication goes out to my wife Beverly—there before the grace of you go I.

PREFACE

If I were to tell you that this book was written by a guy who has only walked unassisted for two months of his life, you'd probably be inclined to assume this to be one boring or sad book. That would not be farther from the truth. Okay, I may have missed a shot at gold in the Olympic 100 yard dash or maybe a gold in the pole vault event, but this guy's life has been far from boring. After all, I did win a huge ostrich race trophy at a county fair once. So thanks for taking the time now to glance through a few pages from my life.

CHAPTER 1

At the risk of losing your interest before we get out of the first paragraph, I feel compelled to at least give you a brief history of where the Harshbarger name came from. Apparently, the name "Harshbarger" was not a long enough name early on. The farther back you go in time the longer it gets. The earliest mention of our family name, that I have found, occurs in Basil, Switzerland, in 1529. Supposedly the name means "Deer Mountain." After some genealogical research, I've been able to trace our family name of "Hirschberger" back through Switzerland to a stout and handsome man, no doubt, by the name of Jacob Hirschberger. I'm certain ole Jake must have used some pretty smooth lines back then like "Ya Der," (?) or "HejSotnos" (Hey Sweetie) and "Jag Ar Singel" (I'm Single) to sweep his girlfriend Maria Petra off her feet. They married and my records indicate that little Christian was born in 1723 to a Jacob (1697-1762) and Maria Eva Petra (Unk-1802) in Epstein, Rhine providence, Bavaria Germany. Christian apparently grew to be a large man and served as a soldier and bodyguard under Emperor Frederick, II "The Great" of Prussia (1740-1786). Christian was later apprenticed as a tailor and made the decision to come to the United States of America boarding a ship named the St. Andrew and arrived on a Saturday, September 9, 1749, from the Port of Rotterdam, Holland.

Pennsylvania German Pioneers: A Publication of the Original Lists of Arrivals in the Port of Philadelphia from 1727 to 1808, Vol. I record for an ancestor

Saint Andrew 1749   397

Jacob Leydig	Jacob Herbig
Christoph Weber	Hans George (H) Garner
Samuel (X) Meyer	Johan Henrich Gerndt
Leonhart Kessler	Valenthein Haag
Johan Petter Druck	Johannes Mellinger
Friederig Neuhoff	Jacob (X) Eshelman
Petter Ihrig	Johannes Jung
Jacob Brandt	Johannes Funck
Johannes Berr	Christian Eschbacher
Ullrich Staufert	Christian (W) Wenger
Daniel Staufer	Hannes Wenger
Daniel Berr	Johanes Brubbacher
Johann Friederich Bohr	Peder Eschelmann
Andreas Keller	Jacob Eimann
Andreas Keller	Christian (X) Frisch
Henrich Caspar Racke	Martin Spreng
Jacob Friedrich Debertshäuser	Adam Helwig
Johannes Corell	Johannes Eppelmann
Johann Engelbert Morgenstern	Hans Jacob (+) Weyse
Peter Willhelm	Johann Adam Dörr
Cunradt Hoffmann	Hermanus Heger
Balser Weinberger	Johannes Huth
Frans Juns	Peter Ahles
Christian Hirschberger	Simon Zeherman
Johan Kuns Heisler	Johann Peter Kramer
Conradt Stichter	Christoffel (+) Henzy
Vallentin (X) Scitter	Jacob Weiss, Senior
Johann Wilhelm Franck	Matheas (X) Weise
Ulerich Hackmann	George (X) Shambach
Henry (X) Stauffer	Johannes Hackman
Aberham Brubacher	Ullrich Jordre
Johannes Walder	Henrich Stauffer
Johan Adam Stahler	Uhellerich (+) Stover
Johann Conradt Seybel	Hans George (X) Hobler

The ship's Captain was James Abercrombie. Christian arrived at the Statehouse in Philadelphia and a deed of September 18, 1757, shows where Christian bought property in Frederick County in the colony of Virginia for 25 pounds. It appears that after arriving in the U.S., Christian started farming. In 1777 he also bought a 25-acre parcel of land and an island in the South River of the Shenandoah mountains.

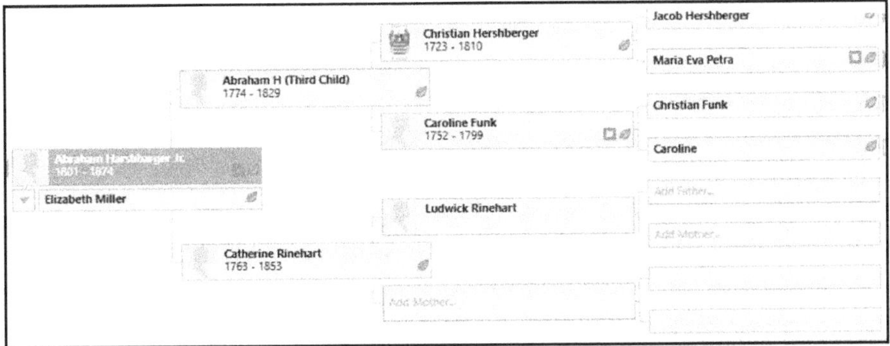

That piece is now in Luray, Virginia, off of New Market Highway and is still owned by the Gander family–after a Gander son married one of Christian's daughters.. That farm is still in the Gander family. Due to English schooling influences, the Hirschberger name was changed to Herschberger. Christian was a busy man having nine children with a lady by the name of Caroline Funk (1752-1799). They then became the parents of Christian, Jr., Susanna Sr., Barbara, Daniel, Henry, Anna, Marie, Elizabeth and Abraham. Christian, Sr.'s wife Caroline died in November 1799–five years before Christian's death. Because he was still so smooth at 73, Christian married again in 1800 to a Suzanna Garmin. This second wife was sometimes listed as Widow Garman. Records indicate that he was a patriot to the colonies during the Revolutionary war. Christian passed away in February 1805 in the town of Plantation – in the county of Shenandoah, Virginia.

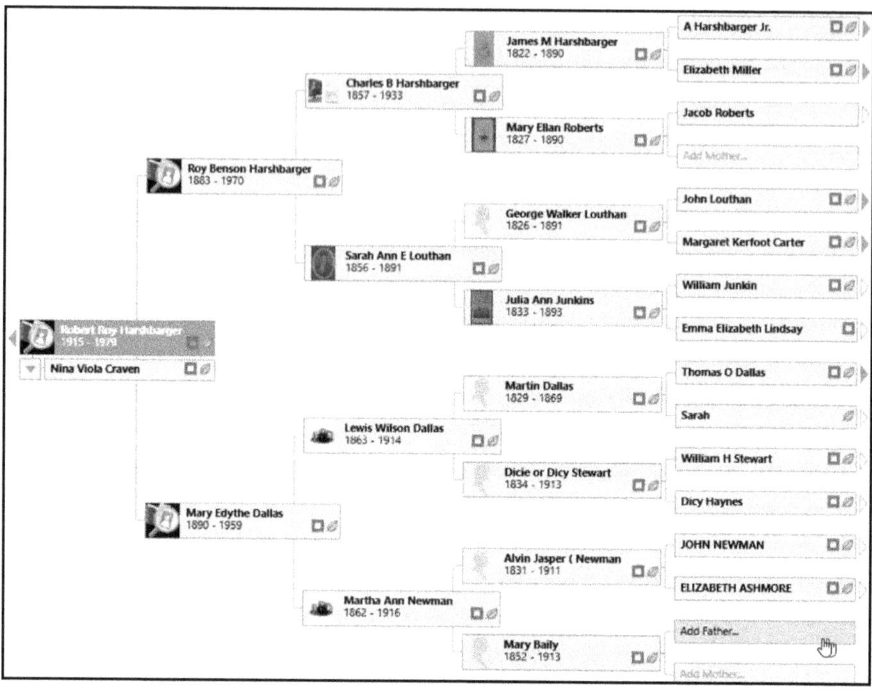

My mother's family name and history that I've been able to find goes back to a Richard Cravens (1630-1676). He had a son whom was named Joseph (1676-UNK) and who fathered a son Robert (1696-1762).

In more recent years, the family has dropped the "S" on the Cravens name and some historical research suggests that the name Cravens means "garlic place." Charming, huh? Reaching back a few hundred years, there is evidence to show that, through her female lineage, my mother's family may be connected to William "The Conqueror" (10-14-1024-9-9-1087) from France–the first King of England. His wife (one of three) was Queen Matilda of Flanders and his parents were Robert, I, of Normandy (1000-1035) with his wife Harlette De Falaise (1003-1050).

Before I get too far back in to the weeds, I should probably tie this little time travel excursion back to the Harshbargers of the 21st century. My Great-Great-Grandfather was no doubt a babe magnet (See Picture) by the name of James Miller Harshberger. He sired Charles Benson Harshbarger (note the evolution of the name spellings) who fathered Roy Harshbarger. He and Edythe were the parents of my Dad Robert Roy Harshbarger, Sr. I am Robert Roy, Jr., and our son is Robert Roy, III.

My mother grew up in Charleston, Illinois, with her parents Thomas and Elizabeth Havens Craven.

Mom's parents with the king.

She was the 5th of 8 children. Way back in her family line you will find William The Conqueror, King of England. Mom always told me that her claim to fame was working in her father's restaurant and serving a piece of pie once to a college student—who later became a well-known folksinger, Burl Ives. Apparently Burl Ives trumped William the Conqueror and the first King of England.

My Dad grew up on a farm between Arcola and Humboldt, Illinois. He started college at Eastern Illinois University which was about 25 miles away in Charleston, Illinois. While in college, he started playing the violin and he also met my mother while spending time in Charleston. My mom was fond of telling the story about how my dad rented a room in a boarding house near them when he was going to college. As Dad would walk by in the mornings, she would say to her mother, "See that guy, right there? That's my man. I'm going to marry him someday." My parents were married in St. Charles, Missouri, on November 21, 1938. Dad was 23 and my Mom was 24.

After they were married, my parents moved into a little 4 room, rural farmhouse about a quarter of a mile from my grandfather Roy Harshbarger's homestead. My Dad was the 2ndof Roy and his wife Edith's 6 children—one of which (Willis) died after just 4 months. Roy farmed 240 acres and was very active in the local Humboldt Methodist Church. Home from the Navy after WWII, my Dad helped his father farm but quickly needed to supplement that income with his own efforts. Over the years, he started buying farm equipment like a tractor, planter, hay baler, combine, a lime spreading truck and so on. He would then start hiring himself out to local farmers for the chores his equipment could satisfy. It was called "custom farming." After a few more years, Dad had the opportunity to rent, then buy, 140 acres of farmland about 3 miles south of Mattoon, Illinois. That farm became known as the South farm and was about 18 miles from our home—making the logistics of time and farm equipment interesting.

It was 14 months after my parents were married that they brought along my older sister Mary. She was born in January of 1940. I never had the nerve to ask Mom and Dad why they waited 7 1/2 years to have me but, sure enough, I showed up on July 24, 1947....a bouncing 10-pound baby boy. All was well for the first 14 months of my life and then I ran in to a little snag. While on a family vacation I became ill with a high fever and my folks took me to a nearby hospital where I was diagnosed with "poliomyeglitis." I was hospitalized for over a year–initially in Barnes Hospital (St. Louis)–and became totally paralyzed. The only memories I have of that involved a spinner toy on my crib and a children's party they "took me down" occasionally to watch the "clowns." I remember being terrified with the clowns. Over time I regained some of the strength in my right arm and left leg. I was told to exercise, exercise and exercise in order to maximize my recovery; then, throughout my life it was suggested that I continue a vigorous exercise program. So I did–swimming, rowing machine, pushing laps in my wheelchair and so on. As it turns out, that was bad advice but no one knew that to be the case at the time.

(Mary and her family)

CHAPTER 2

As I mentioned earlier, I grew up on a farm that was owned by my father's parents Roy and Edith. Initially it was a four-room frame house. They owned 240 acres of farmland situated between Arcola and Humboldt, Illinois. After returning home from the hospital, some strength started to come back in my right arm and left leg. I was fixed up with a variety of orthopedic devices—leg braces, a back brace, crutches, wheelchairs and so on. All pretty exciting for the new toddler my parents brought home. I gotta say though, to their credit, my parents were pretty good sports about the whole thing. In addition to changing my diapers and all the other fun stuff parents do with toddlers, they got to put on braces, take me to physical therapy regularly as well as follow-up doctor's appointments. By five or six, it was beginning to become apparent that using braces & crutches to walk wasn't terribly practical so I started using a wheelchair to get around. That move also saved me a lot of bruises from the falls I managed to do on a daily basis. I learned to make the wheelchair go pretty straight by using my right arm and left leg to push it. Yeah, it looked a little odd I guess but it cut back on some of the hematomas and broken lamps from my falls. It was about this point in my life that I remember being pretty darn proud of my toy six-shooters but was frustrated having no one with which to play cowboys and Indians. I appealed to my mother to make my sister (who was approaching her teen years) play with me. So she did. Mary wasn't happy about it but she did grudgingly agree to be an Indian—feather, not dot. I was indeed grateful but my fun was short lived. Approximately 10 seconds after we began playing, Mary would let me "shoot" her and she would fall down "dead." Thus, she'd tell me that I won, get up and walk away in search of a phone to call her girlfriends. Initially I was disappointed that this play thing didn't last longer but then I told myself what a great cowboy I was, solving the problems of the old west in less than a minute.

Big things happened for little Bobby as he approached the age of 6. My parents added two more rooms and a bathroom to our home. No more heading out to the tiny little house outside and sitting on a board with a hole and spiders in it. Certainly, manageable in the summer or fall but getting to that little house in the winter was a serious test of one's constitution. Now we had our own indoor and heated special room. Also at 6 my parents hired a teacher to start my education at home. Mrs. Davis was one of the kindest ladies I ever knew. Her breath would stop a train but she was so patient with me and got me through the first grade. The next year, I was sent to Humboldt Grade and Junior High School.

CHAPTER 3

After completing the first grade successfully with the help of Mrs. Davis, my parents decided to move me in to the regular school system–second grade for me would now be at the Humboldt Grade School. The school was two stories so on certain occasions a 7th or 8th grader would have to bounce me up or down the stairs on the back wheels of my chair. My teachers were Miss Niemeyer in the second grade and Miss Slover in the third grade–where I finally learned how to spell my last name. By the time I hit the fourth grade, armed with the ability to spell my own last name, Miss Anderson had her hands full. By then I was tying sweet, little Karen Keller's dress bow to her desk seat while sitting behind her. The most memorable incident I have of the fourth grade is a recess in the gym when a little Amish girl Dorothy Hershberger was pushing me at a pretty high rate of speed chasing another friend Mike Carpenter. Mike made a 90 degree turn as did Dorothy and my wheelchair–but I did not. When my head hit the gym floor, I was knocked out cold. Not sure for how long but I'm sure you can guess what happened then. You're assuming they called 911, an ambulance arrived, I was put on a stretcher with a neck stabilizer, I was whisked off to a local hospital 13 miles away and my parents called. Right? Nope, none of that was done. I was told that a 7th or 8th grade student carried me to my 4th grade room and he poured me in to my seat with my head down on my desk. I do remember waking up after some time and trying to focus on Miss Anderson who was teaching at the front of the room. As I lifted my head off the desk, Miss Anderson said something to the effect of, "Well, welcome back, Bobby" and then she told me what she was teaching about at the moment. When my Dad came to pick me up at the end of school that afternoon, Miss Anderson explained to him why I "missed" part of her teaching that day. Dad was pretty matter-of-fact about the matter and asked if I was ready to go. My fifth grade was pretty uneventful except for Miss Lampkin cracking my knuckles more than once with a ruler for a variety of reasons over time...passing notes, whispering jokes to another student or....well, we don't need to get in to every detail here, I'm sure you get the idea. Sixth grade was relatively smooth with Mr. Raines. Looking back, I'm not sure he was a completely happy man. I hope I wasn't the genesis of that but he seemed a bit crabby, to me anyway. In the last two years at the Humboldt school we had different classrooms with different teachers. A couple of incidents stand out. One, not involving me for a change, came about when our science teacher/football coach Mr. Genta noticed Alan. Alan still had the habit of sucking his thumb—even in class. Mr. Genta noticed this seventh grader with his thumb in his mouth, came over to him, took him by the hand, dipped his thumb in a jar of a powdered chemical, sent him back to his desk and Alan never sucked his thumb again to my knowledge. The other distinct memory I have is that of being in Mr. Van's math class one afternoon—sitting behind Mike Carpenter. I was a bit bored and whispered to Mike—asking him if his face was hurting him. He whispered, "No." So, I said, "It was killing me." Mr. Van started sniffing profusely. He asked what I was talking about and that I should share it with everybody. I just said that I had asked

Mike if his face was hurting him. Mr. Van asked why I cared, so I told him that it was killing me. The whole class laughed—except for Mr. Van. He apparently didn't see the humor in the air and he invited me to spend the rest of the class in the hall. I wasn't sure how that would further my math education but I obliged. By the seventh and eighth grade I started to find a lot of interest in sports. Of course, running wide receiver routes in football was limited to some degree by being in a wheelchair. The same was true with chasing down fly balls in baseball. Consequently, I umpired a lot.

Grades nine through twelve had the Humboldt students going to Mattoon High School. That was a bit of a shock with over 400 students in my freshman class alone.

CHAPTER 4

Before venturing off to my college years, I should probably tell you a little about my home life. Growing up on the farm was an adventure for a toddler and young lad in a wheelchair. For the first 6 years of my life we all used the "potty" outside in that cute little, aromatic building that I swore was mainly inhabited by spiders. I would first knock on the door to see if they would let me in. As mentioned previously, when I was six, my parents added on a bedroom and a full-functioning bathroom with indoor plumbing and no spiders. I remember that our homestead consisted of a house, garage, a grain bin and a shed way out on the lot. By the age of 12 or 13 I had saved enough of my own money to buy a rifle. Life could be a tad slow on the farm. By 7 or 8 we had a TV with "rabbit ears" and, depending on the atmosphere, you could get three channels. We also got a telephone installed about that time. We were on a "party line" and 4 short rings indicated that a call was coming in for us. One or two rings meant a call was for someone else on our party line, and so on. Party lines were interesting because you could pick up the phone when you heard someone else get a call–then just listen in. "Ole lady Parks" was always doing that if my friends would call. I'd say "Miss Parks is listening so be careful what you say," and you would immediately hear a "Click!" My Dad was a farmer and was the hardest working man I have ever known. He was also the kindest–and a Christian. I could only hope to be half of the man he was. Dad served in the Navy aboard the destroyer USS Purdy during WW II. He worked in the ship's radio shack. On one occasion, just before shipping out, he was involved in an accident while on the ship's deck when a cable snapped and wrapped around his ankle. The ship left port without him and, while in hostile waters, it was hit by a suicide Japanese plane and all those in the radio shack were killed. I have been forever grateful that Dad was not at his post that day. As I mentioned, my Dad was a terrific example of kindness. He bought a John Deere riding tractor/lawn mower so I could mow our lawn and lots. Also, I used it to ride down the road and mowed a couple of neighbor, widowed lady's lawns for a little spending money. I'd use my rifle to pick off the annoying starlings that hung around our farm trees. Sometimes I'd wheel out to the distant lot and shoot rats as they poked their heads out of the corn shed. One evening, as I was coming back in to our house, I had one bullet left in the chamber. I saw a basket Mom had placed over one of her flowers on the corner of the house and I said to myself, "I'll bet I can hit that without aiming." So, I shot and the bullet did, indeed, go through the basket. However, my sister's dog Terry just happened to display some bad timing by coming around the corner of the house the instant my bullet went through the basket. Well, this wasn't a pretty night for little Bobby. The dog, registered his displeasure, my sister was really angry with me, my Mom wasn't pleased with me nor was my Dad. I'm sure Dad was upset about the dog to a degree but now he had to call the vet out (after hours) and for THAT he was really steamed. Okay, the dog survived so everyone eventually calmed down. I have told you about my Dad, my mother was always very kind to me, as well, but it seemed that she was frequently not what you would call a happy person. She was often suspicious of Dad for no reason and always ready for a big argument that could last for days. After Dad passed on August 14 of 1979 (64), Mom became much more congenial and kind to her primary family. I think Mom may have been somewhat insecure–partly because she didn't finish high school, while Dad attended a couple of years at a university and played the violin as a young man. Mom was more generous also now that she was a widow, living along. I remember on one occasion my wife and I had taken her out to dinner and she said, "You know, when your Dad was alive, we never seemed to have enough money to do anything. Now that he's gone, the money is there but I don't have anybody to do things with. If I paid for airfare and a week stay at a hotel in Hawaii, would you and your Beverly be interested in going with me?" I remember coming back with some smooth response like, "Awwwe, Mom, you don't have to do that but let me check our busy calendar–YEP, you name the time and we'd love to go with you!!" I think the calendar check and my response took less that a second. As I said, Mom was much kinder and more easy going in her later years. She continued to live out her last years on the farm until, sadly, she gradually became overcome with dementia and could no longer safely live alone. My sister and I arranged a place for her in an Arthur, Illinois, nursing home. Mom passed away at the age of 85 on May 19, 1999.

CHAPTER 5

My parents petitioned out of the Arcola school district for me because their schools were all two story buildings. Wheeling my chair in to MHS the first couple of days was like being dropped off in New York City and having someone say, "Ok, now LEARN." There were so many students (over 1200), lots of teachers, tons of pretty girls to impress and tons of rooms and hallways. For this ole country boy it felt like I needed a map–you know, the kind you get when you go to one of those giant amusement parks. I was thrilled that my locker was found to be in the same zip code so I told myself, "You can do this, Bobby!" After a couple of weeks, like everything else, my schedule and the locations of my classes became routine. I still had an interest in sports but, clearly, I wasn't going to make any teams–yet, I still wanted to be a part of the Mattoon Green Wave. So I spoke to the Athletic Director Harry Gaines and told him how I wanted to earn my graduation year numbers (freshman year) for the one side of the "letterman's jacket" and eventually the letter "M" for the other side of my stud letterman's jacket. This kind man took me on as his personal assistant. Besides taking calls and notes for Mr. Gaines, I would call umpires and referees to arrange their attending games on our schedule, then send them contracts. I'd arrange for programs to be generated for each game. I worked as a liaison between the coaches and AD. There were a variety of other duties that kept me busy but it was worth it to get the letter I earned for my Letterman's Jacket–oh, and free admission to the games. I remember being thrilled when I found myself in the senior yearbook picture of the MHS Letterman's Club.

Of course the one thing every teenage boy wants more than anything after reaching 16 is to get his driver's license. After passing the driver's education course and logging enough hours behind the wheel on my permit, I presented myself to the state driver's license office for my official test. I passed the written test in short order and then it was time for the driving part of the test that had to be passed before I could get that coveted license – the card that said I could drive legally...no silly permit anymore. My guess is the license bureau staff drew straws in the back room to decide which sacrificial lamb, er....excuse me, which employee got the job of riding with me as a final test to my driving ability. I mean, what could go wrong? It's just another paralyzed, 16 year old kid, whose right leg and left arm wouldn't work that needed to transfer in to the passenger side of the car, fold up and load his wheelchair in the back seat and scoot over to the driving position. I can still see the guy's worried face– probably wondering if he was going to live long enough to cash in that 401K that he and the wife have been putting back for retirement. I'm actually not sure who was more scared at this point. Sure enough though, I passed the test and returned the poor guy, safe and sound, back to his license bureau office.

I suppose I was an average student in high school. I didn't carry a Mensa card and chose not to join the Latin club – largely because I could barely get through Mrs. Heath's English class. I say Mrs. as an assumption that she was married and, well, because I remember that woman being pretty severe. You can make up your own definition of severe here. I believe she was pretty close to 173 years of age. All that I remember is that she liked to kill me in English class. That said, to this day, I can tell you what a past participle is or a helper verb. You want a sentence diagrammed, I'm your man. It's thanks to Mrs. Heath that today I'm probably one of those grammar Nazis that you learn to hate.

Not sure how you spent your Friday or Saturday nights during your high school years but from 1962-65, in my experience, it was pretty common for guys like me to borrow the family car and go cruisin'. That is, you'd pick up a buddy or two and drive. You put in enough miles to qualify for a small vacation–but in reality, you only drove down two or three streets all night honking, waving, stopping in for a curb service soda at Gills and then start driving again. Very impressive....down Mattoon's Broadway street to 12th street, through Gills (Sometimes for a soda and burger), back up 12th, then Broadway street again, spin through Schick's store parking lot to turn around and repeat the drive all over again. Yep, all that with your favorite tunes playing, lots of waves and a horn toot here and there to other friends doing the same thing. Life was good.

There was one night that especially stood out in this manner of having fun. On this occasion, the night was starting to get late, a few of our friends had dropped out of this cycle of laps around town and as I was starting to drive through town to go home–about 13 miles away, my closest friend Francis was doing the same thing. We only lived about 5 miles apart so we both pulled up to a red light in our respective cars. One of us revved our engine and, of course, the other one responded. Anticipating the light turning from red to green, we both took off with some serious acceleration and–you guessed it–the pretty red lights showed up in our rear-view mirrors. After pulling over, we were "invited" in to the police station to which we considered it briefly, then accepted. I must say, Mr. Policeman was a bit stunned to have me open the passenger door, fold the right front seat forward, pull my chair out of the back seat and then have him pull me up the stairs of the inaccessible police station. Francis and I were duly lectured by an officer as to the dangers and penalties of "drag racing." We both politely agreed with him and were sent home complete with our speeding tickets. The next morning, I shared my criminal experience (and time served) with my parents. My Mom's comment was, "Oh, Bobby, you've just broken your mother's heart." My Dad was clearly upset with the notion that we did this at the stop light IN FRONT OF THE POLICE STATION.

With studying, working for the Athletic Director, selling programs at games, duties at home (and drag racing), I didn't have a lot of extra time or interest in dating yet. The one girl that I did have an interest in was a lass by the name of Susie Best. I dated her a few times because she was–the Best.

CHAPTER 6

To be honest, I was never a great student, nor was I that fond of school. Yeah, I suppose there's a correlation there but, given my physical issues, it was pretty clear that I didn't have a great future in the military, construction work or walking on the moon. So, I swallowed the reality that college would be in my future. Somehow, by the grace of God, I got accepted the University Of Illinois–a Big 10 Conference School–and moved in to one of their dormitories called Forbes Hall.

I had an interesting array of roommates in my years at Forbes Hall. My first was a guy older than I and was named Steve. He was very quiet had very little in the way of a sense of humor. Actually, he seemed more of the mass murderer type. Of course I deferred to him in most all decisions about our room because sleeping with one eye open at night is hard. Starting college was relatively traumatic for this ole country boy. There is the constant pull between having fun, studying and getting to where I need to be when. Let me just add here that I found the ladies of college to be in a whole different genus or league then what I knew about. That was a new frontier that I knew I would want to learn more about too–since I was here to learn, you understand.

I was never entirely sure what happened to my roommate Steve–nor was I sure I wanted to know – but he didn't return to school the second semester. I never saw him again but I DID get a new roommate. His name was Ken. He seemed like a pretty nice guy, easy to get along with. He considered himself a rock musician though I never saw the slightest hint of any talent that would substantiate that claim. The main thing I do remember about Ken was that he taught me a valuable life skill – the "art" of fart lighting. Seriously, I'm not making this up. One night I noticed that our room had a rather pungent smell in it. I remembered thinking that perhaps Ken had a G.I. issue and I didn't want to say anything that might embarrass him. Well it turns out that Ken's bar for embarrassment was set pretty high. Those I knew in the dorm referred to me as "Barger." That night Ken said something like, "Hey, Barger, wanna see me light a fart?" It may not come as a shock to you to know that I had never been asked that question before. With some fear that one spark in our room that night could bring down the building, I responded, "Uhhh, sure." The next scene involved Ken sitting in his desk chair, getting his cigarette lighter out, pulling his knees up to his chest–and then wincing. Eventually, the "situation" presented itself. He put the lighter in place and boom. Sure enough, a flame came out of Ken's pants that would rival the V-2 rocket first used by NASA. I have to admit, for a moment I felt like I might have just been violated but the look of pride on Ken's face assured me that life would go on. This was just Ken being Ken. Little Bobby was learning a lot in college – just in his first year!! I was sure that my parents were going to be p-r-e-t-t-y proud of their boy.

So the next year of college saw me moving back to the university and moving in to the same dorm – but in to a three bed room. Ken remained my roommate and the third guy was named Doug.

Doug was what we would generally consider now as "cool." He was smarter than Ken and I combined (to which you shouldn't be overly impressed), his hair was somewhat long, he was nice looking (based on his dating schedule) and he was, indeed, a drummer in a rock band that played in various campus clubs.... okay bars. I didn't realize that Doug had some talent in agriculture or horticulture as well. One day he asked if I'd like to go with him to "harvest" the crop at his "farm." Of course, I'm still in the "act first" and "think later" stage of my development and said, "Sure." So we drove out to the countryside in his car. Doug pulls over and stops near a patch of what appeared to be weeds. Doug gets out, cuts a bunch of these plants off and stuffs them in his three large coffee cans. Alright by now I had figured out what was being harvested. When we arrived back at the dorm, Doug was proud to show me how these "weeds" were to be cured and would reside in the top of his closet. Doug started as a pre-med student in college but later changed to plant biology from which he obtained his PhD and became a professor, even had a couple of plants named after him.

Looking back, I guess I'd like to think that I'm a lot more compassionate now than when I was an 18 or 19-year-old college student. Pretty much back then in a guy's only dorm, everyone was ARG, ARG, ARG!!!! Sports, beer, somewhat rowdy and just basically full of it. Everyone was treated pretty much the same and any physical disabilities made little difference. I liked that. I liked the honesty, the recognition of having a disability but being treated equally. Such was the case with me and Lester. Lester also had a disability (cerebral palsy) and used a power wheelchair. Everyone in the dorm treated me and Lester just like any other able-bodied guy, which is how it should be. Both Lester and I would want it that way. On occasion here and there if we became bored or needed a study break, my roomy Doug and Lester's roommate (another Bob) would decide to play some football outside on the concrete pads of the dorm. Bob and Lester against Doug and I. Roommates against roommates. Doug and Bob would borrow a couple of wheelchairs. It was to be a tag football game between the four of us. Okay we did have to make some slight rule changes to accommodate Lester's needs. He couldn't catch a pass with his hands so it was decided that if the ball hit Lester's head, that would be considered a completed pass. Also, it was decided that if Lester got his feet stuck in the spokes of the opposing player, that would be considered a tackle. I think Lester was on board with these slight rule adjustments. I think. The guy was not a soft spoken young man. Before you get a sense that we were being cruel, let me assure you that Lester had fun and was all in with these little sport outings. He would, however, occasionally protest vehemently if Bob threw a pass "completion" a little too hard. When that happened we could hear Lester cursing through some distorted expletives.

Okay, I know this sounds cruel, maybe in the range of sick, but before you judge too harshly, let me just say that Lester was on board with all of this and thoroughly enjoyed getting out with the guys and playing sports. The only (twisted) expletives we ever heard come out of Lester was if Bob, his roomy, threw and "completed" what might be called a bullet pass. At the end of our little "game," the testosterone was flowing. We all laughed, slapped each other on the back and had some hilarious stories to tell.

I always wanted to play football – especially in college. The university did have an intermural wheelchair football program and I was lucky enough to make the "Blue" team. With rules adjusted somewhat there were only 6 players on the field at one time. Let me define field here. We played our games inside the Armory where the floor was like hardened ash. I have only two memories of that experience. One is when I jammed a finger trying to catch a pass and to this day that joint soreness still flares up some. Okay, not a big deal except that at least it lets me refer to "My old football injury" today.

Well, throughout the years hence, I do remember jokingly telling people, in an overly braggadocious manner, that my wheelchair was a result of an ole football injury when I scored the winning touchdown. Of course, I always left that conversation with little doubt that I was joking. Apparently that didn't include everyone. On one occasion my oldest daughter Jenny was at a University of Illinois football game with her mother-in-law and at one point she and turned to Jen with a serious look. She asked, "Jenny, does it bother your Dad to come to these football games?" Jenny asked why it would bother Dad and her mother-in-law reminded her of the ole football injury. At that point, Jen shouted, "DID HE TELL YOU THAT????!!!" Later Jenny's report indicted that she took a deep breath and explained to her about her Dad's warped sense of humor.

I should probably pause here and let you know that now, as a Christian, I thank God for each new day and for saving my rear end from some of the incredibly stupid decisions I have made through the years. I'll share some of those as we move along here but I think there is likely no such event or decision that I have made more ill-advised than that of deciding to set what I/we thought would be a world land speed record for a guy in a wheelchair. I'm not sure if any alcohol was involved at the time but some of my brilliant college dorm friends and I were sitting around one evening talking about incredible feats that had been accomplished. It was around 9:00pm in someone's room and in the background the radio was tuned to the Chicago rock-and-roll station WLS with "crazy" DJ Dick Biondi. In all honesty I can't remember which of us four guys, came up with the idea but the next thing I remember is being out at one end of our dorm's two long parking lots tying the front end of my chair up to a buddy's Kawasaki motorcycle. That was done because at high speeds, of course, the front castors of the wheelchair would rattle like your local Kroger grocery cart. Come to think of it, there's an old country music song by the late Waylon Jennings that seems to apply here. It's called, "I've always been crazy but it's kept me from going insane." So now we're all set. My buddy, always thinking safety first, was, of course, wearing his helmet. It never occurred to either of us that perhaps I was the one that should be with helmet but off we go. The first couple of runs only got me up to 25 or 30 miles per hour. Except for hitting a small bump on one of these runs causing my chair to roll on one back wheel only for about 15 feet, we experienced no problems. On the final run, my buddy got me up to 40 mph but the stop at the end of the parking lot was rather abrupt. Abrupt being defined here as having to pry the metal from my wheelchair away from the metal of my buddy's bike, BUT SUCCESS!!! I made the personal declaration of setting the world land speed record for a wheelchair at 40 miles an hour. With a great deal of pride, we all went back to the dorm room, called WLS and gave Dick Biondi our news–then listened carefully to see if he would announce it. Sure enough, on his next break our accomplishment was announced, we cheered then exhaled, probably scratched our bellies and set back with a great deal of pride. Only then did it occur to me that the people financing my college (parents) might attach some other judgment to my feat that didn't include pride. The next day I promptly shared the big news with my girlfriend–later to be wife. She didn't share my exuberance, I think the word stupid was employed at one point and I was told if I ever did anything like that again, we wouldn't be a couple. Well, that played out in an interesting way as you'll read about later.

I met this girl Jan in a basic music class. I knew zero about music except to do a pretty good lip-synch to a bluegrass tune called "Dooley" by The Dillards – also known as "The Darlins" from the Andy Griffith TV Show. This was a very basic music course for credit and I struggled a bit. Apparently, this gal seated nearby took pity on me and offered to help "tutor" me outside of class. It was never clear to me why she took the class because she was already pretty good

with music and able to play the piano. Anyway, we started dating –
going steady to use an old phrase.

On one occasion Jan told me that she was going to visit her
parents 3 hours away and could I take care of her pet gerbil? Let
me just share something with you here. I've never been a big lover
of pets. I just haven't been. I know that's bad. I never really cared
for the trips to the zoo either. However, that said, a guy is going to
do anything within reason to endear himself to his girlfriend, so
my response to the request was, "Of course, I'll take care of that
little rat, er....your pet gerbil for a couple of days." So she brings the
little guy over to my dorm room complete with her winter coat. I
asked if that might be a little big for him and, with an eye roll, was
instructed to throw it over his cage at night to make him sleep. Got it.
Next morning I pulled the coat off the cage and was happy to see the
little varmint still alive. The bad news, however, was that overnight
this creature had chewed a hole in Jan's coat. Great, now there was
an outside chance that I might look bad or undependable to my
girlfriend. So I decided to come up with some story involving the
emotional needs of a gerbil being separated from its loving master
and that,"It was probably just trying to get close to you Jan, and
your scent." Perfect. It was Friday morning and I was off to class.
Home from class by 2pm, I peeked in the cage and terror struck.
The gerbil was walking around on 3 legs–completely dragging his
one rear leg/foot behind him. Shocked and realizing that this might
be a little more difficult to explain away to some emotional longing,
I grabbed the cage, threw it in my car, made a run to the local vet
who saw me right away and said, "What would you like me to do with
this." I asked if setting the broken leg was out of the question. He just
looked at me with eyebrows raised like I had a spike in my forehead.
He suggested that they don't set gerbil legs. Okay, then I guess the
only thing to do is just keep the gimpy gerbil and do a mea culpa.
Wait! There might be another option presenting itself. I asked the vet

if he sold gerbils. He did. I asked if he had one that looked like this little guy – except not dragging his leg/foot behind him. He did. A small exchange of cash (and gerbils) was made and problem solved. On Jan's return I presented the gerbil looking none the finer–this slight breach of accuracy was never discovered. Sorry about the hole in your coat but….

Well, one music class treble clef led to another and in our senior year we were married and moved to student housing. At the time, we had a pretty good relationship except it always irritated me that she was so much smarter than I was. I was what one might call a slow reader. I rarely tackled a book that didn't have lots of pictures and a 20-point font. She could read a book in the morning that would take me a summer to get through. Consequently, she did all her assigned readings, rarely went to class and mostly got A's. I, on the other hand, went to every class or extra credit session and by the grace of God would get a B or C.

Somehow I graduated. I had a bachelor's degree with a major in radio and TV journalism and a minor in psychology. Yeah, I know, kind of a strange combination but when you consider the bright spots (being alive, no criminal record, married and done with school), I was okay with that. So, with my chest puffed out, I took that degree and started applying for jobs–preferably something related to my major.

My first job out of college was that of a radio disc jockey at WIAI, a 50,000-watt FM country music station in Danville, Illinois. It was a noon to 6 PM gig Monday through Friday and 6 PM to midnight on Sundays. With preparation, time that turned into a 42-hour week and an initial paycheck big enough to cover a week of tuna helpers. The first thing the program director, Jim, told me was that my name would never fly on the radio. It had to be something shorter. So the next day I took on the middle name of my great-grandfather Charles

Benson Harshbarger. That was acceptable so forevermore on the radio waves out of Danville, I would be known as Bob Benson.

After a few months on the air, program director Jim, who had the morning show, was talking to someone on the phone as I came into the studio with some of my show preparation. I happen to hear him say, "Oh sure Benson will be glad to do that, just give me the time and place." Naturally my curiosity was peaked so after he introduced his next tune, I asked Jim, "What is it that Benson will be happy to do?" Seemingly to have only a slight interest in my question, Jim said, "Oh, this Saturday you are to go to the nearby Georgetown fair and participate in an ostrich race."

Me: "Wait, what?"

Jim: "Yep. The fair promoters have a company coming in with three ostriches and they want the disc jockeys in town to race against each other with an ostrich pulling your cart."

Me: "Have you noticed I'm in a wheelchair?" Jim: "Yeah that'll be no problem."

So three days later I find myself wheeling into the Georgetown Fair-grounds thinking what could possibly go wrong with me in an ostrich race. I was directed over to the racetrack where, sure enough, there was a collection of three huge birds that the attendants were seemingly having problems keeping under control. One of the promoters directed me to a cart tied directly behind one of these 230-pound birds. Three well-built men were struggling to hang on to the bird who was clearly impatient and ready to run. Another DJ was in the cart next to me. His name was Rich and we looked at each other with eyebrows–raised as if to say, "What in the hell have we gotten ourselves in to!" A third station's DJ was invited but didn't show. He likely was the Mensa card carrier of our three local radio stations. So, Rich climbed in to his open-air cart and I transferred in to mine. The instructors told us that,"These birds can go from 0-50 mph in three steps...so hold on." No Duh. He gave both Rich and I a broom. I asked if this was to clean up after the bird or me. "No, no," he explained, "this is to help you get the ostrich to turn. As with any race on an oval track, you always want to turn left. Thus, to scare the bird in to turning left, you hold the broom up to the right side of its face and shake it." Obviously a highly engineered strategy after years of fine tuning. So, armed with my broom, the guy holding the gun asked if we were ready. The fairground stands were full and the PA announcer was hyping up what was about to happen. The men holding the birds let go of the birds just as the starter shot his pistol. My ostrich took off like a bat out of hell. Same with Rich who was on my left. The jolt and speed at which these birds took off might be compared to that of being shot out of a cannon. The first tactical move for me was to jettison the broom. My goal at this point had changed from winning to still being in the cart alive at the finish line. As my bird approached turn one, he apparently wasn't well versed on race etiquette, and he made a sharp left turn on his own. All I heard from Rich was a terrified scream of, "Ahahh@#$%$#@!!!!." What little time I had to think between prayers, the question occurred to me, "How does one stop this bird?" Again, that little matter hinges on the concept of scaring the bird. The fair personal and ostrich racing promoters all stood in a row at the finish line jumping up and down, hollering and waving their hands. Sure enough, my ostrich slowed and pulled up, then stopped as the promoters grabbed on to him. I had won the race-thanks to cutting off Rich on one of our turns. I was presented with a huge, 3' tall, wooden and gold trophy etched with "Ostrich Racing Champion Of The Georgetown Fair, 1970. To this day I still have that trophy.

My fame as the county ostrich racing champion was short lived. As a country DJ Noon to 6pm I was called upon by a local promoter to MC shows involving country music stars. The shows were presented in the local high school auditorium that seated about 750 people. Some of the stars that I got to meet and introduce on stage included Dolly Parton, Dave Dudley, Jesse Colter, Chrystal Gale and Waylon Jennings. Think early 70s folks. Okay, like any good host might do, I did some homework and came up with a few pretty good jokes to open the show and tried to loosen up the crowd. My theme song to open and close my radio show was a violin version of "Greensleeves." So when the announcer said over the public address system, "Ladies and gentlemen, from WIAI radio, Bob Benson," the performers' band would play my theme song and I would wheel out on stage and give the stock pitter-patter of, "Hi, everybody, great to see you all here tonight. We've got a terrific show lined up for you in just a few minutes with (insert star/s name) and while they're getting ready, I gotta great story to share with you." At that point, I'd go in to my carefully prepared jokes, in the form of a monologue. Nothing. There were 750 sets of eyes just staring at me and you could hear a pin drop. There was zero response. I've been at wakes that had more laughter than this. Speaking of wakes, I was dyin'. Finally, I introduced the star and the show took off. A few months later I was again asked to MC a show with another Country Music star. Initially, my thought was, "No Way!" Then a light went on inside my brain – It's because of the wheelchair!!! The jokes were good, it was the chair that stunned the crowd. They have been listening to the voice of Bob Benson regularly on their radio but obviously had no idea that he was in a wheelchair. Plus, there's the little matter of Mom and Dad drilling in to you growing up that you're not supposed to laugh at people who are different or in a wheelchair. I need wheelchair jokes to put everyone at ease. Trust me, there are not a lot of tasteful wheelchair jokes just lying around out there. I did manage to come up with a couple to open with and one of my own. So now, when Bob Benson is introduced, I rolled out, "Hello, everybody, we want to welcome everyone tonight and....." I decided to face this little wheelchair issue right up front. I thanked them for listening to my show in the afternoons and acknowledged that they must be a little shocked when the guy behind that voice is in a wheelchair. I would say, "That's okay, you know lots of people asked me if I was born this way and I'd tell them, "Yes and how shocked my mom was when the chair came out first.'" I'd follow that up with a couple of other wheelchair jokes and then use my material from the previous show. This time they laughed hardily at those same jokes. Success! At that point I introduced the star and the show was successfully on its way.

Because my life wasn't complicated enough at this point, a buddy and I decided that it would be a good idea to buy a go-kart and race it at the local" Thunderbird" race track. He would be the mechanic, I would be the driver. Solid plan. Turns out there were a couple of speed bumps in it. First, after we spent the money on the kart, tires and engine work, there was no money left for a helmet. After a couple of weeks and enough money for a helmet we were in business and ready to race!! The other wrinkle in our goal of racing fame was speed. The maximum speed of our little kart was around 75mph. Now that might not sound fast but when your rear is 4 inches off the ground, it feels fast. That said, the other karts were doing 80-85mph. Lesson learned, when money and time are limited, do not go in to an endeavor that takes a lot of both. You would think I could have come up with that before jumping in with both feet but.... I/we won zero races in the year and both my friend and I decided to re-boot our life plan....Nice way of saying that we sold the kart AND my helmet at a discount price.

After two or three years, it became pretty clear that a local DJ job in Danville, Illinois, was probably not going to be enough to allow my wife and I to start a family. Wait. We had ALREADY started a family. We learned in 1973 that a little girl was on the way. Sooooo, the search began for a medium market station that needed a DJ. Doing a search like this is not cheap. You have to drive to the medium market city, have an appointment and then do an audition. Decent DJs are a dime a dozen so one really needs to stand out. On my first such audition in 1974 I visited a station in Wisconsin. The program director instructed me to introduce two records, read a commercial and read some news copy. The guy on the other side of the window from the studio I was in (the engineer) pointed to me and then started recording. It seems like I got through a couple of record intros and was reading a commercialcial when all heck broke loose. President Nixon had been told by the Supreme Court to release his Watergate tapes and they had just been dumped to the press. Bells went off, lights were flashing all over and you can sense people running around in the station's like maybe the building was on the verge of collapse. Stunned, I stopped my audition and asked the engineer what was happening. He told me the story and that discussion was quickly followed up by the program director who came in and said, "Mr. Harshbarger, just a piece of advice. When doing an audition tape, you never, ever stop it because of what's going on around you." He thanked me for coming and said that they would call me. That, of course, is universal speak for "Get out of here, you're not getting hired." It was at that point that I decided radio would not be my primary career. Let's see, what could I be when I grow up? Construction worker? Astronaut? Indy 500 race car driver? After a long discussion with my wife who gave me a serious dose of reality, I turned those options down. I had a minor in psychology in college, perhaps that was my destiny–to go back to school. Not being a typical scholar or someone who enjoyed school, I wasn't thrilled with this option but decided to pursue it. I quit my DJ job, re-enrolled in the Social Work Masters program at the University of Illinois and visited the local Department of Veterans Affairs Medical Center. There, I spoke with the social work chief, Frank, the guy was saint. He agreed to hire me as a social work associate until I got my degree 18 months later. The schedule was a brutal one working 3 days a week at the VA and driving 90 miles round trip three days a week to attend 5 classes each day at the U. of I. Time flies when you're that busy so the 18 months went by pretty quickly and, with graduation, I became a certified MSW social worker working full time at the VA Medical Center. God's timing is good. It was in January of 1974 that my wife and I welcomed our first baby girl, Jennifer. Up to that point in history I think it's not hyperbole to say that she was the cutest and sweetest baby known to modern man.

Daddy

CHAPTER 7

So, now, I guess I'm officially an adult. I have a job, wife, child and bought an inexpensive two-bedroom little cabin on a lake. The job was a good one. Initially I worked on two floors of the four-story acute medical unit. I was more than a little busy but enjoyed my job, worked with some terrific people and I learned a lot. If there WAS a little wrinkle in the job, I'd have to say that it was the dreaded pager. That tiny device has to be one of the most hated inventions for mankind, I believe. It could interrupt nearly everything you were doing with another assignment and it kept you in a continual state of running behind. That said, it didn't take long for this new college grad to figure out the one GOOD thing about the pager. If one were to set it up right (Ohhh, like buying the ward secretary a Diet Coke), one might get paged a half hour in to the boring, weekly 90-minute staff meeting. Of course like a good Social Worker, I would have to respond immediately. That little exercise went on for years without the Chief or Assistant Chief questioning it; however, after a few months of my pager going off after 30, 40 or 50 minutes in to the meeting, I noticed a collective eye roll from the rest of the staff as I left.

On one occasion, while returning to my office, I came upon our pathologist who was apparently just entering his lab to do an autopsy. Nice fellow and we both spoke. Then he said, "Hey, Bob, would you like to come in and watch an autopsy?" Me, "What?"

The pathologist said, "Yes, I'm just starting, come on in, grab a robe watch carefully."

Well, to be honest I'm thinking how careful do I need to be here given the situation but said, "Uhh yeah, ok, sure, I'm in."

Not for the faint of heart but it was a fascinating experience. Trust me, it was a lot different than the frog exercise we've all done in high school biology.

After a few brief years in the acute medical unit I was transferred to the psychiatric unit of the medical center. I was the social worker for two wards and shared patients with other social workers on the locked ward. No problem, right? I had a lot of psychology courses in college. Wrong. It was, initially, a vastly different experience for me interacting with those struggling with severe psychiatric issues. It required a speed course on appropriate responses. For example, from day one on the psych unit, I was greeted by an older feisty gentleman named Alfonse with, "Hi, shithead!" He held on to that moniker for me for a couple of years, until he was discharged. I tried to get him to at least say Mister Shithead once without success. On the second day of my tenure on the psych unit, I received a referral of a new admission assigned to me. I went down to the locked ward to do my part of his evaluation and saw from his chart that he was a 36-year-old male just admitted that morning. So, I entered the locked ward and called out for a Mr. Smith (?). A guy sitting on the back of a couch raised his hand so I approached him with, "Hi, Mr. Smith, do you have a minute I could talk with you?" His more than appropriate response was to look around the room, then look back at me and say in his best sarcastic voice, "No, I'm pretty busy right now." Of course I thought to myself, "Well played, Bob." One time around Christmas I had a holiday decoration taped to my office door. It happened to be closed on one occasion while I was working on some progress notes. Suddenly I hear a RIPPPP!!! I thought, "Someone just ripped off my door decoration." I went over to open the door and saw one of my outpatients running down the hall WITH my decoration. I yelled Harold, "Bring that back here!" He continued to run away but responded with, "I didn't take anything." On the way home that night, I saw Harold walking down main street – with my decoration. Another moment that stands out from my time in psychiatry was a personal one.

It was at about this time in my life I had decided that I needed to exercise more. So I started swimming at the YMCA before work. The Y didn't have seats in their showers and I was reluctant to shower in my wheelchair giving me a wet seat the rest of the day. So I would take a bag to work with dress clothes rolled up in it and shower at work. My office was directly across from the patient bathroom and showers. One day I did my swim thing, came in to work a half hour early, showered and transferred back from the shower in to my wheelchair. As I'm stark naked and drying off, a nurse came in with something to be deposited in the dirty laundry, looked at me, said, "Hi, Bob" and proceeded to exit the bathroom. Of course I was stunned, felt maybe I should smoke a cigarette (even though I didn't smoke) and would only look down at the floor when that nurse approached for the next month.

To get serious for a moment, I think I mentioned before that I was a Christian, and I believed that I was; although, looking back, I think I may have been simply following on with the traditions that I grew up with. I honestly couldn't really say that I felt close to or communed with God. My wife and I went through the motions of church and I just, well, believed, in some impersonal way. It was in December of 1976 when that changed. My wife was pregnant with what was to be our second daughter. On the big night of December

13th she went in to labor and our second daughter, Mandy, was about to be born. Delivery was after midnight, I think around 1:00 AM, and Mandy was wrapped and placed in a tray while the doctor worked on my wife. I happened to notice that this very small baby was retracting upon trying to breathe. I pointed this out to the doctor who immediately ordered that the nurse take her to ICU. The nurses there worked on this child–struggling with everything in her to breathe. Eventually the doctor came, did an exam and ordered a stat consult with the chest and pulmonary specialist – at around 2:00am. That doctor finally arrived in the middle of the night and worked on our Mandy a bit, spoke with the pediatrician and nurses, then left. Mandy's color was turning gray and dusky. Eventually the staff left her and a nurse came out to us as we were watching through the ICU window. She suggested, "Why don't you two go back to your room and we'll let you know when it's over." Devastated, we weren't sure what to do, except cry. Then one of us suggested that we call our pastor, Paul Stern. I did that and he said that he would be right out to see us – it was around 2:30AM at this point. When he arrived, we took him down to the ICU window and Mandy was still fighting for life but looking very dark and more dusky than before. Pastor Stern turned to my wife and I and said, "Let's pray." We readily agreed and held hands. The pastor's prayer asked God to let His will be done...that we were turning this situation over to Him and if it be acceptable to Him, we ask that HE let this child live. It was immediately after he said "Amen" to this prayer, that the three of us turned back to look at our sweet, young daughter and SHE HAD TURNED PINK!!! That is the absolute truth, and we were stunned. The nurses that had "abandoned" her were shocked and returned to start working with our baby again and the doctor couldn't believe it. She told us that Mandy still had a problem with her breathing (a collapsed lung) but that she had called Riley hospital for children out of Indianapolis, about 85 miles away. She said that a Dr. Costello would be in charge of the pediatric specialist team. After about 90 minutes, I remember a team coming in with haste and one lady was barking orders out right and left. I thought a Dr. Costello was coming so, like an idiot, I approached the lady who was barking orders and introduce myself as Mandy's Dad. I said, with some disgust, "So WHERE is Dr. Costello??" To which she said, "Sir, I'm Dr. Costello." At that point I removed my chauvinistic self from the situation offering something lame like, "Oh, sorry. Carry on." After awhile she said that if we wanted, we could start heading toward Indianapolis and that they would eventually pass us by ambulance. That's exactly what happened. In the wee hours of the morning, on a dark 4-lane highway we saw red lights way behind us. "That's our Mandy," we said. As the ambulance approach our vehicle, we flashed our lights, they pulled up beside us and turned their internal lights on. We could see Dr. Costello waving at us with one hand, smiling and helping Mandy breathe using an ambu bag with her other hand. After arriving at the hospital, the staff worked with our precious new daughter and eventually the doctor came out to tell us the wonderful news that Mandy was breathing well on her own now. She had encountered a mucus plug in her bronchial tubes that would inflate and collapse her lungs then cycle through again as she struggled to gasp for air. That "plug" was dissolved and she could breathe independently now. Praise God. In a couple of days, we brought our new daughter home. More than ever now we believed in God, prayer and miracles.

BABY
VIOLET
TALCUM POWDER
NEW YORK
ANTICIPATION

CHAPTER 8

So as 1976 came to a close, I looked around and saw a growing family. As much as I loved our home (surrounded by trees and a lake with bass fishing available) it became clear that our little two-bedroom cabin was shrinking. After giving it a lot of thought, my wife and I decided to buy a lot in the country from our family physician. The area was called Indian Springs though I confess that I never saw an Indian the whole time we lived out there. We had a basic three-bedroom ranch built and before you knew it, we learned that our family was to grow even more when our third daughter was to be born in September of that year, 1979. That year was filled with many, many mixed emotions. Besides the excitement of a new little girl (Megan) coming in to our family, and moving in to a new home, I also learned that my Dad had cancer and not long to live. I so wanted him to meet Megan but the timing was going to be close. Unfortunately, Dad passed away in August of 1979 and Megan was born in September of that year. I have to admit that I struggled greatly with the loss of my Dad. He was such a kind man who absolutely loved his children and grandchildren. Gradually my grief was taken over by a flood of joy as we welcomed little Megan in to our family. Delivery went well and, in all modesty, she was as cute as could be with her big, charming eyes.

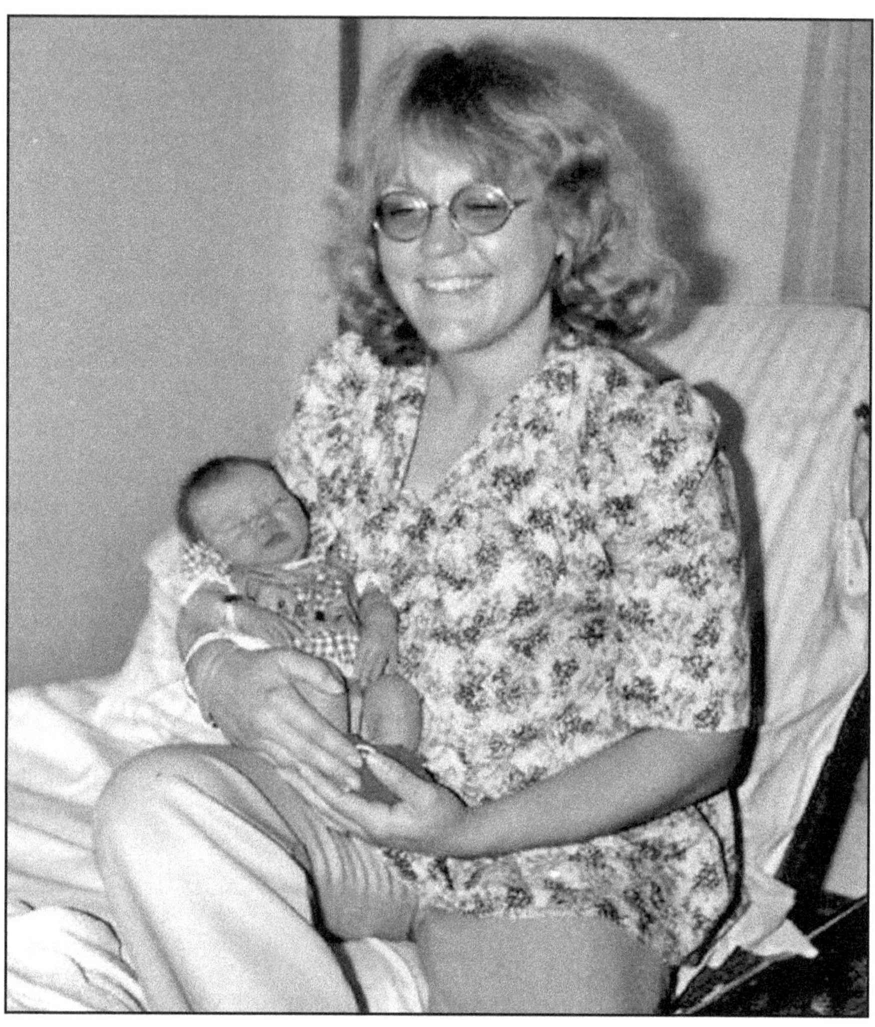

Her sisters loved to dote on her as well as her parents. Our family was complete – or so it seemed at the time. I felt close to my girls and their own unique ways. Of the three, it was Mandy who would crawl under the car with me to "help" change the oil or mow the yard on our fancy red riding mower.

After awhile, I felt myself missing radio. I contacted another of the stations in town – WDAN – and went in to interview with their program director, another Bob. I landed a four hour/day Saturday and Sunday job there. Bob Benson – aka Mother Benson's Boy – was on the radio again playing some light pop music. I remember that at this point in the industry, it was seldom that the DJ would cue up records. Everything was moving to the digital age. You would introduce a record, push a button and somewhere out in the control room, the music would start playing. Okay, occasionally the two would get out of sync and you'd look like the village idiot but that was rare. Frequently, we would tape our show also – especially if it were the weekend early sign-on shift. You'd have the sheet with tunes that the computer had set up to play and you would simply tape what you had to say in your various talk positions, introducing the next tune or reading a commercial and so on. One of the strangest things about this setup, for me, was hearing the DJ on the radio and suddenly realizing, "Hey, that's ME!" On more than one occasion I would wake up to the radio alarm clock and hear a bright, perky, good morning voice saying stuff like, "Hi everybody, Bob Benson here to get you up and going on beautiful Saturday morning...." Of course, with everything being digital, it was important to label whatever work you may have taped—whether it be reel-to-reel (back then), a cartridge, etc. On one occasion I was assigned a 30 second commercial to cut. I went in to the production room, grabbed a reel-to-reel (again, back then) tape and bulk erased it with a demagnetizer. I cut the commercial, transferred it to cart, got back in to the studio just in time to kick off my show and all was good. I thought. During the show, Bob the program director popped in and out, frustrated, asking if anyone had seen his taped interview with famed baseball announcer Harry Carey. Of course, no one had and then I was overcome with this sick feeling in my stomach. Eventually I worked up the courage to ask him if it was on this certain reel-to-reel tape in the production room. He confirmed that yes, that was the tape, "Have you seen it?" I was forced to tell him that not only had I seen it, I erased it! It was unlabeled so I bulk erased it and put this shiny new commercial on it. "Wanna hear it?" You would have thought that I had hit him in the forehead with a brick. He became apoplectic. He stuttered and said, "You di didid what?" I explained what had happed again and, no, he didn't indicate that he wanted to hear my new commercial. He said, "How could you DO that?" My response, perhaps, could have been a bit more sensitive but I said, "It was easy, I just took the bulk eraser, went Bzzzzzz on the tape and it was gone." I DID note that the tape had no label on it but I'm not entirely sure it helped his mood.

CHAPTER 9

Yes, life was good with our family of five...for a few years. That said, unfortunely, we come to a point in my life that still brings sadness to me. Carelessly, my wife and I began to slide away from some of the fundamentals of our church and the factors that are so important in a good marriage. We both made some bad decisions and without going through the details of fault on both our parts, our marriage ended with divorce in 1982. We sold our home and I moved in to an accessible, two bedroom apartment. I missed my family dearly. I was able to have my girls 33% of the time, enjoying every minute with them. The mornings I had my girls, I was up early to bathe, dress and then start calling out one girl at a time. We would hunker down on our living room floor – in front of the TV with MTV blaring away....I can't tell you how many times we watched Michael Jackson sing & dance to "Thriller" or Boy George pump out "Karma Chameleon" while I brushed their hair. Sometimes we watched taped shows like WKRP or The Andy Griffith Show on our rented VCR. Piece of cake, right? Actually, it wasn't bad – not bad as long as I had a case of something called "No More Tangles." This assembly line would see one girl finished and sent to bathe and dress while girl number 2 was called out for the next dose of the miracle, no tangle hair spray. That process continued until all three of these gals with long blonde hair were dressed, primed and ready for school. Then it was time for one of Dad's hall of fame breakfasts – milk, donut or toast & jelly or waffles & sausages from the frozen food section at the IGA. It's with some reluctance that I pass along this next story from that time period. Hoping that the statute of limitations has passed, I'll take my chances here. A lady friend down the street had a schedule that complicated taking her 5 or 6 year old daughter in to daycare AND make it to work. She asked if I could take her daughter as I took my girls in to drop off at the same place. I said sure and each morning this darling little girl would run up the sidewalk to my apartment and bust in the door. She got to the point where she could hit the door at full speed and simultaneously turn the door knob – at that full speed! After two or three times of that, I cautioned this little towhead to PLEASE come and knock on the door when she arrived. Or, if not knock, please gently open the door and come in. I explained each time that her entry was a bit rude but, more importantly, she could injure herself OR injure someone on this side of the door. She never changed her mode of entry. Frustrated one day, I locked the entry door, heard her little footsteps racing up the side walk and then BAM!!!!! I unlocked the door and let her in. This poor thing was clearly stunned but she was fine and she always knocked before entering from that point on.

Our meal choices for dinner were always a selection of TV dinners (favorite: Salisbury steak) or a variety of Chunky Soups. I would make sandwiches for the girls and me as a satisfying, gourmet lunch and in my OCD state would make them up a month (?) at a time. Then I would put them in the freezer, taking them out week by week.

After about 15 years in the VA Hospital working in Acute medicine, psychiatry and extended care, I was transferred to the

Outpatient/Admission area of the medical center. I absolutely loved working in this area of the hospital and was gradually assigned more and more duties. In addition to my admission and outpatient clinic assignments, I was assigned a few ancillary duties as well – computer (IT) Coordinator for Social Work Service, the Visual Impairment Service Team (VIST) coordinator, the Spinal Cord Injury (SCI) coordinator, the Prisoner Of War coordinator and the Lodger Program coordinator. Our VA had a ward set aside for veterans who had some logistical problems trying to keep their outpatient appointments because of travel problems; so, instead of forcing them to get a motel or sleep in their car, we would lodge them overnight – complete with meals. I began to find that the duties associated with all these coordinator positions started to compromise my true assignment of serving veterans in the outpatient clinics and admissions. In hopes of getting a little relief I discussed this matter with my chief and he re-assigned the POW coordinator position to another social worker. Now, before you feel too bad for me and all these coordinator assignments, I should probably point out that the American Association Of Spinal Cord Injury Psychologists and Social Workers sent me to their annual (educational) convention in Las Vegas–for 19 years straight. Yes, that was a tough assignment but I felt it was my duty to take one for the team, God and country. Did I mention that every year this four-day convention was held at what was then the Riviera Hotel on the Las Vegas Strip? Yes, there are numerous stories I could report from these particular trips but probably those are better left for another whole book someday.

Socially, I spent about a year of hit and miss relationships. At the VA Medica Center, I lunched almost daily with Warren, a Physician Assistant co-worker that told me about a nice divorced lady with two young sons and was a neighbor of his. Her name was Beverly (it still is) and that was in the fall of 1983. I boldly suggested that he invite us both to dinner some evening and he agreed that such would be a good plan. Well that never happened so I eventually called her one evening and we talked for over an hour – eventually setting up a time to get together for our first date. After a few dates we seemed to get along well and decided it was time for me to meet her boys. Josh was four and Chris was nine. I can tell you that Josh was pretty accepting of the situation – much more so than his brother Chris. The first time I met Chris, he came out with a bag over his head. The second time I met up with Bev and her boys was a Bar-B-Que outside. Bev had the ribs and potato salad along with other delicious treats and about a minute after we all gathered around the picnic table, Chris put some potato salad on his spoon, and flipped a spoonful of it on to my shirt. Being pretty observant, it occurred that I had a lot of work ahead of me if I was to bond with this child. That said, I'm proud of both of us for coming to terms after a few years and our relationship can only be described as good, given some time together.

We talked for close to an hour and it felt like a fit. Not wanting to rush in to anything, we dated for a year…I finally hinted at something long term (Okay, I didn't want to buy a ring and have her say no) and the answer I received was the equivalent of, "It's about time!" We married in 1984 and combined our two families. This picture was on our wedding day with our children and both of our Moms.

I must say here that, after accepting Christ, this was the best decision I have ever made.

Did I mention that while we were dating, I was driving a sexy, dark blue Camaro that I was SO proud of? Probably the all-time favorite vehicle I've ever owned. Black leather seats and so clean. One evening as I was leaving Beverly's home, Jenny felt ill. Beverly told me that I should take a plastic bag on the drive back to my apartment and I thought that was a good idea. Well, about half way home Jenny told me that she was feeling really sick, I gave her the bag and she started vomiting like I've never seen anyone vomit, I mean ever. I re-assured her, put my arm around her and told her not to worry – that I hoped she would start feeling better now. We arrived at the apartment, I sent her in with her sisters and picked up the scary bag. Gosh it seemed pretty light, I thought – oh wait, it had a hole in the bottom of it, the contents of which were on my Camaro's floor. My timing has never been great. After checking on the girls and getting them to bed – with Jen feeling better – it was clean-up time. Then, soon afterwards, there was this little neighbor girl I agreed to drop off and pick up at the day care center close to my job. One afternoon, after picking up this little one, along with my daughter, we were driving home in that Camaro I had just cleaned up from Jenny's illness and suddenly the girl said, "I gotta poop Bob." I told her to just hold on – that I would have her home very shortly. That didn't impress her and, in more of a panic, elevated voice saying over and over, "I gotta poop, Bob, I gotta poop, I gotta poop!!!" I believe it was right after I said, "We're almost there" that there was this explosive and volcanic eruption of diarrhea from this sweet little girl. I wasn't sure how someone could live through that – and the ending of this movement wasn't quick. I called her mother suggesting that she might want to come out to my no longer fancy Camaro and take her child.

Well, enough about my favorite car. Bev and I continued to date and after about a year God blessed us with our marriage in November of 1984. With her two sons, and when my three girls were present, we had a pretty full house.

Meanwhile, after 4 years of a part time (8 hour/weekend) gig on WDAN, we had a new program director. Rumor had it that the station was about to go a different direction – syndicated news/ talk instead of music. With that in mind, I asked Greg, the current program director, what this meant for me and my two 4 hour shifts. He asked when I had planned to go on vacation, I told him in a couple of weeks and his response was, "Okay, then just don't come back." He noted that the station owners are changing all the station's formats over to talk radio. After Greg "released" all the on-air personalities, the owners then released him. So that was it, more free time on the weekends for me, my bride and new family.

CHAPTER 10

Adjusting to our new blended family presented some uhhhh, exciting situations from time to time. Five children in our three-bedroom house made it cozy. Of course each child had their own set of activities and friends so we were seldom lacking for something to do or somewhere to go.

(Bev's two boys, Josh and Chris)

Relatively soon after we were married, I traded my sexy, dark blue Camaro in on a typical "Dad" car – a brand new Olds Cutlass Ciera. Pretty nice vehicle. All shiny with that new car smell. I remember driving it home and showing it off to our children. After the "Show and Tell," we all retreated in to the house. After awhile, Beverly and I noticed that her son Josh (5) and my daughter Megan (4) were missing. So, we did what every other dedicated parents would do and fist bumped each other screaming "Peace and quiet!!" No, no....they both came in to the house soon after our search for them began. They were all excited. They wanted us to follow them outside. We did so and they proudly showed us how they had "washed" our brand-new car with a few paper towels and a little water. They had just left a few scratches (among the streaks) and only a small dent on the hood when they had climbed up to reach a few tricky places. As a parent, I have to tell you there are moments when you absolutely cannot say what you're feeling. Sometimes you eat the statements that are on the tip of your tongue and you just hope God quickly gives you words of praise and pride in all your kids hard work.

Somewhere in 1995 I bought a shiny, new, red Monte Carlo. That wasn't big enough to take our family of seven anyplace without making multiple trips – so we also bought a used seven passenger, powder blue, Chevy station wagon. Of course, I mostly "let" Bev drive that monster around so it quickly became known as the "Bevmobile." One advantage Beverly DID have with the powder blue wagon was that the kids that were driving seldom asked to borrow her car. That tank was a lifesaver though when it came to vacations. We could load up all seven of us, a wheelchair, countless suitcases and head out of town in style. Well style may not be the exact word I'm looking for here but we had some good times as a family in that wagon. I remember one vacation driving through North Carolina on our way to Virginia. We happened to stay in Ashville, North Carolina. Beverly had expressed some interest in seeing The Biltmore there. That's a beautiful and huge mansion on a 4000 acre estate built by the Vanderbilt family. So we pull up at the gate and I ask the gentleman how much a ticket would be to visit the mansion. He told me $45 each. It was late afternoon. I did another quick count in the back seats at $45 a pop, added that to Bev and I, then said to the gate keeper, in my best Arnold Schwarzenegger, "We'll be back." And I was right, 30 years later Bev and I went back indeed for the tour.

The years began to slip away all too quickly. There were many little things that I remember as funny but nothing major to report that would be worth taking your time here. Little things like Bev's seven-year-old son Josh working on a sucker and the family dog Holly showing interest. So as Josh turned to walk down the hall I heard him say, "Okay, Holly, but just one lick." Holly was a huskymixed dog that was strong. One snowy morning Josh asked if he could take Holly for a little walk around our cul-de-sac before school. Bev and I were having breakfast so we said, "Sure." Sitting at the table by our large window, the next thing we see is Holly dragging Josh around on the snow on his belly holding on to the leash. Bev dashed out to rescue the boy before the dog could reach he street.

Bev's oldest son, Chris' wedding was another fun outing in my memory bank. The reception included some karaoke after the ceremony. I remember being encouraged to try something – even with zero musical talent. So, in the interest of being a good sport, I agreed but felt I needed something that would draw the attention away from my lack of vocal abilities. Got it!! Remember Robert Palmer? He was one of those "Blue Eyed Soul" singers with hits from the late '70s to 1990. I picked his Grammy award winning hit from 1988 called "Simply Irresistible." That song included the "Robert Palmer Girls" dancing behind his vocals. If you haven't seen them, these are all attractive women with jet black hair pulled tightly back. They all had bright red lipstick, serious expressions and danced in unison. Of course, I negotiated with my three beautiful daughters

(Jenny, Mandy and Megan) that if I was to try my first time ever karaoke performance, they would need to help me – dancing in unison with serious faces behind me. With just a little practice they agreed and I think, thanks to my girls, we pulled it off without me making a complete fool of myself.

For a few years Bev and I had wanted to have a child of our own. Two attempts failed in miscarriages but finally Beverly had a successful pregnancy with a healthy 10-pound baby boy. We named him after me – so Bobby, the third.

We have a number of funny stories about little Bobby. One that jumps out at me was when he was four years old. The three of us were at the local mall and he decided that he needed to go to the bathroom. Of course, the mall bathroom was in the food court so we sat at a table while he did his thing. That morning Beverly had dressed him in some easy pull-up pants with just elastic around the waist. It was around Noon so the food court was crowded. We waited for a while and just as I had decided to go check on him, Bobby comes walking out of the bathroom area, squinting and rubbing his eye and yelling, "Mom, I pee'd in my eye!!!!" Like an idiot, I said, "What??!! How did you do that?" He proceeded to tell me, "Well, I pulled my pants down from the top and let go by accident so...." You can figure out the rest from there – however everyone in the food court laughed hysterically. Bobby had a few other embarrassing moments for us when he was little but, probably, none more funny than the one in his short "career" in T-Ball and Little League. Bobby seemed a little slow getting his bat around. I worked with him some at home teaching him how to "choke up" on the bat handle. So at his next game Bev and I are sitting in the stands with probably 50 other parents. Bobby is up to bat and, again, it's taking him what seemed like 15 minutes to swing the bat around. Sitting on the front row, I yell out to him, "Bobby! Choke up, Buddy, choke up!!" He turns, stares at me, then starts coughing like he's got a fur-ball caught in his throat. Of course that triggered a roar of laughter from the other bored parents sitting in the stands with us. Thank you, Bobby...another proud moment. Bobby added a whole new dimension to our lives. We essentially started all over again, in many ways. For example, daycare, school, homework and so on. Ironically, our youngest child before Bobby was Megan. When she was a senior, Bobby entered the first grade. That translates in to Dad going to parent-teacher conferences for 34 consecutive years.

As time went on, I still felt the tug of radio. After a chance encounter with the manager of another local station while at Steak 'n Shake one evening, our discussion ended with his comment that I should apply and help out their current morning show jock at the popular radio station known as D-102. After some discussion with my wife, I applied for and got the job co-hosting the 6-9am morning drive show – now it was Scott and Bob in the morning– Mother Benson's Boy was back on the air.

So for the next, almost four years, my Monday–Friday days consisted of getting up at 4am, arriving at the station about 5am, doing some show prep with jokes or interesting news stories and what ever else was needed to kick off our show at 6am with the "Odd Fellows" TV show theme song. We would introduce ourselves as Scott & Bob (aka Mother Benson's Boy), give the usual pitter-patter of time, weather, what's coming up and so on. We had some interesting bits from time to time. We had a contest once where people would call in doing their best rendition of the "Barney" (purple dinosaur) theme song. We called the White House while on the air trying to talk to the President. We were told that he was busy–so we offered them a Scott & Bob T-Shirt, and were shocked that we still didn't get through to the President. One Valentines Day we had a contest to set up a date with our engineer. That went well until we learned that Garret was already married. Sooo we awkwardly gave the date prizes to the winner, minus Garret. Of course every morning we also had prizes for the winner of our "Cheap Thrills and Big Deals" trivia contest. Scott & Bob was a good show based on our ratings. We were the #1 morning show in Danville and one or two years we were rated #1 in both Danville and Champaign/Urbana 35 miles away. The program director whined to the station manager (Mike) regularly that we talked too much and needed to play more of the music. Of course Scott and I stayed with our usual format (that was a proven success) and that ultimately got us our pink slips. That happened to be on my 50th birthday, by the way. I was offered a job back on the AM side with our sister station; however, after nearly 4 years of this brutal schedule, I decided to turn down the offer. After the change was announced to the public, there were numerous complaints in the form of calls and letters to the editor about our dismissal. The good news, however, was that after almost 4 years, I could sleep in until 6am. Up to this point, my schedule had been to report to the station just after 5am, leave the station at 8:45am (taping the last 15 minutes of our show), dash to the VA Medical Center by 9am, work there until 4:30 as a Social Worker, then return back home at 5pm....5 days a week.

Ironically, my wife had planned a surprise 50th birthday party for me the weekend before Scott and I were told that our morning show had been terminated. People from the medical center AND the radio station were invited but the manager "couldn't make it." It was a great party. That afternoon Bev sent me on a drive to pick up the baby sitter on the notion that we were going out for my birthday. I returned home with the sitter and everything seemed normal until I opened the door to rooms full of people yelling, "SURPRISE!!!" Lots of people showed and after a couple of hours, I heard the theme song Elvis Presley used at his concerts. And then, sure enough, an Elvis impersonator walked through the porch door complete with guitar and a white jumpsuit. He opened with "That's Alright, Mama" and the party went in to high gear. At one point a couple of ladies threw themselves at "Elvis'" feet and were rewarded with silk scarves from the king's neck. A great night, indeed, with friends and much fun.

The time-line gets a little fuzzy but sometime long before all of this I noticed some weakness in my good arm and leg. I had bought a rowing machine to work out for a half-hour in the mornings. One morning I noticed that a gallon of milk seemed heavier than usual as I pulled it from the fridge. I blew it off as an anomaly or just weakness from the exercise. The weakness, however, didn't go away over time and so I went to see a neurologist. After a number of tests, he diagnosed me as having postpolio syndrome. That's a condition that involves a progressive weakness of muscles throughout one's body because of the initial virus of polio. That virus "killed" a number of nerves that control one's muscles. Other nerves try to "move in" to the areas of loss over time to compensate for the lost nerves–then, over time, with activities of daily living, exercise, etc., those nerves trying to compensate with their extra load begin to fail. This eventually led to a number of lifestyle changes. With my shoulders becoming "over-worked" using countless strokes daily to push my chair, I decided to get a power wheelchair. Of course you can't fold or get a power wheelchair in to your sedan, so it became necessary to purchase a van – not just any ole van for $35,000 but a van that has a ramp in it that will fold and unfold at the push of a button. That bad boy adds another $20,000 to the price for the original vehicle. Still, I was independent and able to drive myself to work and around. Handy, but this arrangement did present some image issues. On one occasion I left work early to go see Bobby in a junior high track meet. As I pulled up to park, there were these three GLMs (Good Looking Moms) nearby chatting with each other. So what was I gonna do? I hit the button, the van door opens, the ramp unfolds down to the ground and I roll out in my power chair then close the ramp. The ladies stared the entire time. As I rolled by them I spoke, and they spoke back but had the look on their faces as if they had just witnessed the parting of the red sea. Of course I told myself that they were just stunned at my good looks and hot body... that the ramp had nothing to do with their stares. So, then I find a place to "sit" in the stands. I settled in just in time to see little Bobby run the 880-yard race. He started with every one else but as the winners crossed the finish line, Bobby was no where in sight. I kept looking for awhile then FINALLY I spotted him running by himself toward the finish – alone – then smiling and waving at me in the stands. As I waved back I noticed the other parents were staring at me–again. Proud.

Let me say here that all our children turned out exceptional in our eyes. They are all professionals (teacher, social worker, physical therapist, chef, credit card investigator and military officer) and we are proud of them all. Looking back, I'm amazed at how fast the time has gone. I would do it all over again if I had the chance. By the age of 58 I was down to one job and preparing to retire from that – after 31 years at the Department of Veterans Affairs as a Social Worker.

It seemed like the last 10 years of our family life had included a vacation to someplace in Virginia. To this day, if the word "battlefield" comes up my daughters Jenny, Mandy and Megan go in to a PTSD fetal position. We toured so many that I thought they would enjoy another one. Huh, who knew. Anyway, about 5 years before we were both retired (Beverly 5 years after me) we bought a three-bedroom home in Williamsburg, Virginia. We love it here spending approximately nine months out of the year in Virginia and the other three months in our Illinois home. Currently we have our three sons living in Illinois, a daughter near Los Angeles, a daughter three hours away in North Carolina and a daughter 45 minutes away in Yorktown, Virginia. This is a picture of our family prior to 2013:

THE WHEELCHAIR

In addition to the references that I've already mention about a life in a wheelchair, I'll offer a couple of examples to show you how irony and humor are likely going to be a part of your life, if you learn how to "roll" with your situation.

If you are in a wheelchair, flying presents a whole new and different set of opportunities for humor. First off, almost 100% of the time if you fly in a wheelchair, you are the first on and last off. On one occasion our plane landed on the tarmac and didn't approach those corridors from which to unload or exit the plane. After all of the passengers had left the plane via the steps, the attendants transferred me from my seat to an aisle chair – then the problem of getting my body down the steps to my wheelchair on the tarmac. So the two male flight attendants looked at each other, turned me around so that my back faced the steps, I was tilted upside down so that my head went out first and I was looking straight up at the sky. One attendant had the handle of the chair above my head and the other held the handle by my feet. That attendant looked a bit uncertain of the situation with one hand on the aisle chair by my feet and his other hand holding on to the steps' rail. After a couple of shaky steps, I jokingly asked, "Hey, have you guys ever done this before?" Little did I know I was setting him up for this response, "No but I stayed in Holiday Inn Express last night." That was a popular commercial at the time. Incidentally, I landed safely.

Another funny flying experience. My wife and I flew from Virginia to visit our daughter's family in California. In this new era for terrorists, plane security, etc, TSA is diligent about security – as they should be, of course. Well now when you show up at security, the able-bodied person goes through the stand-up scanner on to the other side. When they see you in a wheelchair approach, they typically point at you with a wand and say, "You, over there." They then call someone else to check you out. Oh no, not with a wand.

This special TSA guy (woman for the ladies in a wheelchair) will feel you all over. Yes they check out the chair but first they feel your tummy, feel your back, they have you tilt to one side to check your right butt, then the other side to feel your left butt, then they feel all the way down both of your legs individually and FINALLY, he says to me, sorry but I need to feel your personal area and starts to feel my crotch. I nearly made a joke and ask him how long he could do that, but have learned that not all TSA agents have a sense of humor. After a brief feel in and around my personal area, the guy leaned over to my ear and said, "You're gonna owe me a drink after this." We both laughed and I was on my way.

Finally, in the vein of our discussion here about life from a wheelchair, I present the:

Top 5 reasons to enjoy being in a W/C

5.) Bar drunks hardly ever call you out for a fight.
4.) When there's a cat burglar in the neighborhood, you're never a suspect.
3.) Children find you fascinating.
2.) Your shoes last a lifetime.
1.) You never have to worry about becoming disabled - ending up in a wheelchair.

So let's be brutally honest. It's hard to really like someone who is always complaining and feeling sorry for themselves, right? Oh you may "have" to like that person because you're expected to but generally individuals aren't drawn to people that are always negative. Yes, it may be hard but, trust me, your life is going to be much fuller if you can move that attitude in to the positive or even present an occasionally humorous demeanor whatever your circumstances.

So much for the lecture.

I have been truly blessed if anyone ever was. God has, indeed been good to me. I'm in the twilight of my life at this point with a loving wife, six successful children, multiple sweet grandchildren and lots of close friends. Bev and I are in love after 35 years, we have a strong faith in God, we are warm, safe, dry and if I had the chance, I'd do it all over again because – it's been a pretty good ride.